The Girl from Chimel

·

Rigoberta Menchú

WITH Dante Liano

PICTURES BY

Domi

TRANSLATED BY David Unger

A GROUNDWOOD BOOK
HOUSE OF ANANSI PRESS
TORONTO   BERKELEY

A mis nietos:
Alejandro, Diana, Ulisses, Aura,
Leonardo, Ismael, Dalia y Cabiria
— Domi

Text copyright © 2000 by Rigoberta Menchú Tum and Dante Liano
Text copyright © 2000 by Sperling & Kupfer Editori S.p.A. for *La Bambina di Chimel*
Illustrations copyright © 2005 by Domi
English translation copyright © 2005 by David Unger from *Li Mi'n, una niña de Chimel,*
published by Alfaguara Infantil in 2003.

Groundwood Books / House of Anansi Press
720 Bathurst Street, Suite 500, Toronto, Ontario M5S 2R4

Distributed in the USA by Publishers Group West
1700 Fourth Street, Berkeley, CA 94710

Library and Archives Canada Cataloguing in Publication
Menchú, Rigoberta
The girl from Chimel / Rigoberta Menchú ; pictures by Domi ; translated by David Unger.
Translation of: Li Mi'n, una niña de Chimel
ISBN 0-88899-666-7
1. Menchú, Rigoberta–Juvenile literature. 2. Mayas–Guatemala–Juvenile literature.
3. Maya authors–Guatemala–Biography–Juvenile literature. I. Unger, David II. Domi
III. Title.
PZ7.M53Gi 2005   j868'.703   C2005-900656-0

The illustrations are in oils.
Printed and bound in China

Table of Contents

The Girl from Chimel

*"Once upon a time there was a girl
named Rigoberta..."*

I'D LIKE TO BEGIN my story like this, the way our ancestors
told their tales — sitting around a fire with the wood blazing,
the flames lighting up their faces, sparks bursting in the air,
spreading heat everywhere. Perhaps if I begin like this, I'll
become a little girl again and return to the village where I was
born.

I am Rigoberta. Chimel is the name of my village when it's
large, and Laj Chimel when it's small, because sometimes the
village is large and sometimes it's small. During good times,
when there's honey and the corn is so heavy it bends its green
stalks, when the yellow, green, purple, white and multicolored
orchids bloom, displaying their beauty, then my village is big
and it's called Chimel. During bad times, when the river dries
up and ponds can fit into the hollow of my hand, when evil
men walk the earth and sadness can hardly be endured, the village becomes small and is called Laj Chimel.

Right now, I'm remembering Chimel…

Once Don Benjamín Aguaré, a wise elder from my village,
said to me, "We look out for one another on Mother Earth."

Right now, I'm remembering Chimel…

There were many wise elders in Chimel. I say *were*, because nowadays there are none. My grandfather was an elder. Let me tell you about him.

My Grandfather

M Y GRANDFATHER came to our village one hundred years ago. He came by foot from the far-off place where he had been born, but never lived.

The people from his village were walkers. They loved to walk and walk and not stay in any one place. That's why they had no land, only footpaths. They were truly walkers. They'd show up wherever there was a festival. They were early risers who preferred to walk the wide and narrow paths early in the morning. They always found time to stop on a hilltop, sit down and count the stars rushing to set behind the mountains or beginning to rise. The people from my grandfather's village appeared everywhere. They were called the *chiquimulas* because they came from Chiquimula, which means "goldfinch." The village got the name because goldfinches were everywhere. This is what Don Juan Us Chic, another Chimel elder, told me.

My grandfather walked and walked. What was he looking for? No one knows. He would swallow trails and leave behind the remains of goldfinch songs. What was he looking for? A mountain that changed colors? Perhaps. Lands that sprouted flowers, strong trees and huge ears of corn? Maybe. But what was he really looking for? Some thick clouds wandering about with their own songs and whistles? Perhaps. A transparent air, a refreshing rain, a sky so blue it was nearly black?

He found a treasure — not a pouch of gold coins or precious stones or a wad of bank notes. No. He found something far better. He found a delightful girl, a bit plump, with a little face, round as the full moon. He fell desperately in love with her. This happened very near Chimel. He hadn't even reached Chimel because it had yet to exist.

So he went to see the young girl's parents to ask them for her hand in marriage. Her parents saw my grandfather in his wide-brimmed straw hat, wearing an Indian outfit consisting of a black jacket and a pair of red pants, lamb or goatskin sandals on his feet, a dark face and white teeth.

"You're from Chiquimula," they said. "You're like a goldfinch flying from branch to branch, never settling in one place." This is what the young girl's parents told him. "No, we won't give you her hand in marriage. We don't want her to become a wanderer like you, wearing a black coat, red pants, having a dark face and white teeth. We don't want to see her wearing a red and black *huipil*, her hair braided with colorful ribbons. We don't want her to become a goldfinch, dazzled by her own chirping and not wanting to work."

My grandfather became very sad when he was told he couldn't marry her. But he was a *chiquimula*, a goldfinch, and soon he started chirping and the sadness passed.

It definitely passed when he carried the young girl off. He went to the fields where she was picking corn. He was riding atop a beautiful brown stallion with a golden mane. He galloped across the field, opened a path through the stalks and scooped up my grandmother by the waist.

"You're coming with me!" he commanded, as he hoisted her into the air.

She wanted to say yes, but couldn't. Fear seized her throat.

That's how my grandmother and grandfather got married. They weren't old as they are now — toothless and walking with the help of a cane. They were two brave people, full of strength and energy. And so they escaped from a village of big trees and rode off on the back of a chestnut stallion, till they reached a place called Chimel.

It had a crystal clear river, and you could see smooth, multicolored stones at the bottom. Fish swam in the transparent water of its pools. The frogs, the long-legged toads and the dazzling snakes enjoyed life together, eating crabs. You could see your face reflected in the smooth river mirror. To the sides you could see fields teeming with fruits, trees and nourishing medicinal herbs. And where the fields came to an end, a huge mountain rose up that was blue in the morning, green at noon, chestnut-colored in the afternoon and blue once again during the cold, star-studded night. And all the while crickets, toads and enormous frogs shook the night as they rehearsed their songs.

"This is it," Grandfather said. "This is the place where I'm going to build a village of one hundred houses and one hundred cornfields, for one hundred families from the four corners of the universe — the yellow, black, red and white."

The air filled with song, the wind with pollen, the trees with birds. The hills were transformed into temples covered with strong, vine-covered trees, and the stones became majestic altars. So many flowers sprouted and Ajaw, the Maker and Creator, blessed the trees, the stones and the multicolored flowers for generations to come.

My grandfather founded this village, and in this village I was born. I, whose name is Rigoberta.

My Grandfather's Stories

M<small>Y GRANDFATHER</small> built houses and planted fields with
his strong hands. My grandmother helped him with
everything in the fields and in the house. They had lots of children who grew up like ants — like fire ants marching up and
down the hills, working at their parents' sides.

When children are working, everything seems so big to
them. A pickax was like the cross that Christ carried during the
Holy Week processions. They had a hard time with the rakes,
because the teeth got caught in roots and large rocks. And if
they tried to turn over the earth with their shovels, they flipped
over and landed on their faces, with chunks of dirt in their
mouths. Still, they kept on working.

My grandfather became an old man in a split second. Just
yesterday he was the gallant young man who had carried off my
grandmother. But the sun had hardly dropped behind the horizon and risen again with its rosy cheeks, and he had turned old
and wrinkled, with calloused, badly scarred hands and white
hair.

That's when he began telling stories to his grandchildren

and their friends. Grandfather knew many stories because he had traveled around so much.

We'd ask him, "Grandpa, why are there white, black, red and yellow people — people of so many different colors?"

"Because Ajaw, our Maker and Creator, made some people out of white corn and others out of black corn. He made still others out of red corn and he made us out of yellow corn and that's why our skin is yellow. Ajaw wanted us to be as different as the colors in the field."

Late in the afternoon, when the sun turned orange at the edge of the horizon, and the cold would make our noses run, Grandfather would sit at the front of the house and tell us old stories about our ancestors. I especially liked the story of the weasel and the hen. It went like this:

"Once there was a weasel that stole chicks and ate them. The weasel scurried about, sniffing the forest ground, when suddenly his sharp eyes focused on a chicken coop full of hens and chicks. The weasel shot off like an arrow, full speed ahead, and leapt into the coop. He threw up a flutter of dust and feathers and cackling, terrifying the hens. He then seized a chick in his claws and rushed off with the loot, leaving the mother hen crying for her lost baby.

"Since this often happened, one of the hens finally said, 'This weasel isn't going to get my chicks! But how will I stop him?' She stayed up the whole night trying to find a way to teach the weasel a lesson. The following day, when the other hens woke up, she gathered them together to hear her plan. She told them about it and they approved enthusiastically.

"That same day, the weasel was snooping about the chicken coop. He wasn't surprised to see a handsome and delicious-looking yellow chick — the fattest chick he had ever seen. Without pausing, he leapt toward his target like a pebble flung from a slingshot. To his surprise the chick didn't even try to escape. The weasel grabbed it in his claws and took off toward his den.

"But the weasel didn't get very far. The chick stuck to his paws and wouldn't let him escape. The weasel was desperate. He tried everything, but no matter what he did, he couldn't run away or shake off the chick. He tried and tried for a good while, until he fell to the ground exhausted.

"What had happened? Well, the hens had constructed a fake chick. Very carefully they glued chicken feathers to a big rock, so that from a distance it looked real. And then they used vines to tie the rock to one of the chicken-coop posts. They smeared the chick with sticky pine sap and the weasel got stuck. When he fell on the ground, the hens drew near and formed a circle around him and began cackling. The roosters started crowing and even the little chicks began peeping together. Everyone joined in the singing. And they sang and sang and sang, running around the weasel, until they too were exhausted. The weasel couldn't understand the language of the hens, the roosters and much less that of the baby chicks. He was so humiliated that when he finally got unstuck, he never ever returned to the coop."

Grandfather knew the tales of our ancestors, going back to the time when white temples rose up above the earth under a white sun. He knew of the Spaniards who had arrived and filled our green, mountain-rimmed valleys with their white, red-tiled houses.

Since all people are alike, Maya tales are similar to those of the Spaniards. Since all people are different, the stories of the Spaniards are different from those of the Maya. For example, the Spaniards believe that there's a place called hell where the devil lives. The Maya believe in *Xib'ab'a,* which is a place where

17

the evil lords live. To combine these stories, my friend Luis says
that "hell begins in *Xib'ab'a.*"

One of the Maya stories that my grandfather liked to tell
was the one about the rabbit without a tail. It goes like this:

"Do you know why rabbits have little cotton balls instead of
tails and why mice have bulging eyes and smooth tails?

"Well, you should remember that long ago, when the world
was bright and shiny and everything was new — oh, so new —
there lived two boys. One was named Jun aj Pu and the other
Ix B'alam Kej. When these boys became young men, they pre-
vailed over the evil lords, the rulers of *Xib'ab'a.*

"These two boys were sent by their grandparents to protect
the first cornfields on the earth. Every night animals would
come and eat all the corn, so someone would have to keep
guard over the fields when the sun left and the moon came out
in the sky. Their grandparents said to them, 'You two keep an
eye on the cornfields. Don't doze against the trees, don't hide
under the stones. Just scare off the animals when they come
near.' This is why even today, in Chimel, the children watch
over the cornfields.

"So the two boys went into the fields and waited for night to
come. The sun went down behind the mountains, and a little
while later the round moon bathed the landscape in white. Jun
aj Pu yawned. So did Ix B'alam Kej. Before an hour had passed,
they were yawning the way caged circus lions roar. Then a lead
blanket dropped over their eyelids and they fell into a deep sleep.

"They had no idea when and how the animals drew near.
Deer, rabbits, snakes, gophers, hogs, mice, hens, monkeys, pec-
caries, even alligators and crocodiles appeared. And all you
could hear was the *crunch, crunch, crunch* and the *chew, chew,
chew* of corn kernels while the boys snored to their hearts'
delight under a tree.

18

"Let me tell you something. Back then rabbits had large, fluffy, white tails, almost as big as the tails of baby horses. And the mice were cute, nicely formed animals, with little, fluffy tails, just like their buddies the rabbits.

"The following day, when the boys woke up, they saw a devastated landscape before their eyes. There wasn't a single cob left, not one kernel of corn. The animals had eaten everything up! The boys broke into tears.

"'What are our grandparents going to say now?' they cried. Still, they decided to go home and tell the truth.

"Their grandparents smiled as the boys described their failure.

"'Instead of punishing you,' they said, 'we're going to give you another chance. Tonight you'll go back into the cornfields and do a better job of scaring off the animals.'

"That night, the boys went back into the fields. The sun set behind the mountain, which resembled a gloomy bull's black hump, and soon the fields were lit up by the soft light of the moon's white face. The boys hid themselves in the darkness.

"A little after midnight, lions, monkeys, tigers, cows, snakes, birds, wild boars and other animals rushed into the cornfields making a racket. This time, however, the boys were wide awake. They pulled dead branches from a nearby tree and leapt into the middle of all of the animals, screaming and shouting, swinging the branches left and right.

"Scared, the animals scampered away. A rabbit ran off to the left of Jun aj Pu, who grabbed it by its large, fluffy tail. It struggled mightily to escape, but its tail broke off in the boy's hand. At the other end of the field, Ix B'alam Kej grabbed a mouse by the throat and squeezed tight. That's why mice have bulging eyes. The mouse also tried to escape and almost slipped free, when Ix B'alam Kej grabbed it by the tail. Since a mouse's tail is very slippery, it managed to get away, and Ix B'alam Kej was left with a handful of hairs. That is why mice have smooth tails and bulging eyes, and rabbits have little cotton balls instead of tails."

These were the stories grandfather told us while we sat outside the house, or by the fire, on those nights when sleep covered our eyelids, making them heavy as lead. This has been happening to children since the beginning of time. Grandfather knew these stories from the Popol Vuh, the sacred book of our Maya ancestors.

The Wandering Piglet

CHIMEL went through a real birth. Everything had to be set up — everything was new. The river where the people went to wash themselves in clear water was new. The glorious sun in the bluest sky of all was new. The white, round clouds, plump as the women in the marketplace, were new. New was the transparent and pure air that sometimes hurt to breathe. The houses, the lands, the seeded fields were all brand new.

When my mother was a little girl, she took a piglet as her pet. Other kids chose puppies, kittens, birds or even turtles. But my mother chose a baby pig. She took him everywhere with her, pulling him by a string, not caring if people laughed their heads off when they saw a little girl dragging a baby pig down the dirt roads of our village.

She took good care of him. Once a week she'd bathe him in the river. Though he kicked and screamed as if being tortured, she soaped him down, rubbing and scrubbing him with a loofah. Then she'd run a bristle brush over his skin until he was clean and pink, as if he had walked out of a book. She dried him with a shawl her mother had knit for her. But the piglet wiggled out of her hands and got filthy right away, for a pig is nothing but a pig. He wasn't like a dog that comes out of its bath and begins to shake like an earthquake, wetting everyone around it.

She would often take the piglet for walks in the mountains. Together they would climb the Chimel mountain which was covered with flowers, trees, plants and bushes. This is also where the *nahuales,* or spirits, sleep and rest, where Ajaw, our Maker and Creator, keeps watch over things and blesses the entire universe. My mother knew all the mountain paths, and she would pull the piglet along. Together they would go up the narrow little footpaths till they reached the very top, where the wind was cold and turned cheeks as red as apples.

One night a strong wind began to blow. The whole family went to bed early and huddled under their blankets. The wind howled through the village, and the tree branches made a shushing sound. Every once in a while there was a banging noise when something fell. When something very big fell, down it went, *kerplunk!* You could also hear windows blowing open and closed. The loud wind scared everyone.

The coyotes came down from the mountains. Coyotes are like very wild, mysterious dogs. Though they are friendly, they can also be fierce and dangerous. They like eating hens and other household animals. The good thing is that they usually stay in the mountains, hiding under rocks or in nicer places. And at night when the moon is shining, you can hear them howling in the distance like suffering souls. But they're a nuisance when they come down to steal farm animals. And they can be a bit frightening, because sometimes they attack people as well.

That night the coyotes took advantage of the gusty, noisy wind to sneak into the village. From far off you could hear the chickens fussing and cackling. The villagers thought that the wind was disturbing them. My mother tossed and turned on her straw mat, unable to sleep. Despite the clatter of the wind, she heard footsteps near the pigsty and a piglet's cry splitting the darkness.

"Coyotes," my mother thought. She got up, ran to the door. When she opened it, she saw a pack of them escaping toward the mountains. In the darkness she could see one of them had a piglet in its snout. Without thinking, she grabbed a club from the floor and ran after the coyotes. Her parents ran after her, but it was too late. They only glimpsed her tiny shadow merging with the forest's darkness.

"The coyotes are going to end up eating her as well," they thought.

It was useless to look for her. The cold, dark wind of the night knocked off their hats, blew out their *ocote* torches and hurled leaves against their faces. They were unable to find her. My grandparents returned home miserable, convinced that they had lost their little girl.

But the following morning, my mother came down from the mountains, carrying the baby pig in her arms. All by herself she had confronted the coyotes with her club and frightened them off. Then she had sought refuge under a big rock and spent the night drifting in and out of sleep, waking up every once in a while to make sure her pet was all right.

The whole village was awed by her courage. Our elders said, "This is a good sign. She'll grow up to be a brave woman who will survive many challenges. She should thank her *nahuales* and they in turn will give her strength and wisdom and will protect her memory forever. Her sons and daughters and grandchildren will all be courageous. When the day of *Toj* arrives, she will return the piglet to the mountains."

In time we would see that the elders were right.

The Plants and the Forest

From the time she was a child, my mother loved to sneak into the forest and talk to the plants. The flowers, the green leaves of the trees, the mosses and the lichens all have a language of their own. They listen and understand. They shrink and wither without anyone to love them. When they hear gentle words, they grow big and strong. And they also have secret powers.

The forest was full of trees, vines, orchids and all kinds of other flowers and plants that block out sunlight. It was always dark, and for this reason a bit scary. My mother loved to pick orchids and hang them on the monkey tree bark, where they'd extend their roots and grow beautiful flowers. She would go deep into the forest and while gathering orchids, listen to the secrets of the plants. Amid all nature's noises she'd hear heavy tree branches falling in the distance, as if in a dream; the songs of strange birds in the treetops grazing the sky; the *tick tock, tick tock* of the woodpecker, who was our best friend. That's how she discovered that many plants can cure the illnesses of men, women, children and old people.

Years later, when I was a little girl and if I were ill, my mother would force me to drink herbal teas made from the weirdest plants. If I couldn't fall asleep, I'd be given a drink of *chipilín*, a sweet-tasting plant. If I had a stomachache, she'd make me a hot broth from the *altenxa* plant. Soon my stomach would stop hurting.

But there were other plants with even stranger names that cured me better than the medicines from a pharmacy. There was *xew xew*, which got rid of headaches and eye strain. There was *saq ixog*, which was also good for the stomach, and *chilacayote* leaves, which helped heal foot injuries. *K'a q'eyes* was great for curing colds and flus, while *sik'aj* would force terrified worms out of my stomach.

My mother inherited this plant knowledge from her grandparents. When she was quite young, she began to heal her Chimel neighbors.

When she grew up she became a midwife — a woman who helps other women have children — since there were no doctors in Chimel. It's a wonderful vocation. It's all about welcoming newborn babies. A midwife helps mothers give birth by lifting their small, pink babies out of them. When a baby comes out of its mother's womb, the midwife slaps the baby's bottom and it bursts into tears. This means that the baby is healthy, its lungs are working, and it has what it needs to breathe well. Then she washes it in warm water and dries it, and puts it fresh and clean into the mother's arms. Of course it's a beautiful vocation! That's why our neighbors in Chimel and the surrounding villages really loved my mother. She would help them, many of whom she had welcomed into life.

Nowadays kids are born in hospitals, but in Chimel they are still born at home.

Grandfather and the Cornfield

W HEN MY GRANDFATHER became an old man, he was once more a child. Like the children, he had to watch over the cornfields so that the animals wouldn't go in. Grandfather would hide against a rock with a stick in his hand. Little by little, he built a roof out of palm leaves, and by using a few sticks as support, he built himself a little hut by the side of the cornfield. If animals came near, he would yell or chase after them with a stick, frightening them away.

We children would help him because he would tell us stories during his free time. For example, he told us the story of the little man who braided horses' tails at night. He was a *nahual,* a source of power. Sometimes the little man would be a *duende,* a good spirit, and at other times he'd be a demon.

Grandfather would tell us that this man was as tiny as a child, no bigger than two feet high. And he had a huge hat on his head, the kind that cowboys wear in Mexico. He had eyebrows as thick as whiskers and whiskers as huge as eyebrows turned upside down. He was as small as a frog, and the only nice part about him was his pair of big black eyes.

He fell in love with all kinds of women, but because he was so small, none of them loved him back. This made him so angry that, at night, he'd slip through the stable walls. And he'd begin to braid the tails of the horses. (Grandfather talked like people from the olden days. He'd say old-fashioned words like "braid" or "knot" or "augur.")

So some mornings, the few horses in Chimel would end up having braided tails. The women would cross themselves and the men would make jokes. No one knew if someone had done it as a prank, or if the little man with the big hat had stopped by the night before.

Grandfather also told us that each thing had its *nahual*, its shadow, its double. The earth, the tree and the mountain all have their own spirits. The earth has its *nahual*, the rocks have their *nahuales*, the mountains have theirs, our ancestors have theirs, all people have *nahuales* — the sun, the animals, the winds and the air have *nahuales*. That's why you need to talk to the earth, the river and the flowers. That's why you have to respect them. You have to ask their permission in the same way that you ask people for permission. When we cut down a tree, we ask for forgiveness. We have to do it. When we go into the mountains, we also have to ask for permission.

We live together with nature — inside nature. We are part of its energy, its force, and we need to invoke its spirit. We can't live fighting nature. That's what Grandfather taught us under his palm-roofed hut while he rolled a cornhusk cigar and smoked it.

"*Thmoking*," Grandfather would say, with a strange accent.

And all at once he'd rush off because he had seen a mouse, a snake, or some other wild animal go into the field to eat the corn. Screaming and shouting and waving his stick — that's how Grandfather frightened them away. Then he would explain that animals, like people, are greedy. They like to eat more than they need. And that's why they came to steal the corn.

Grandfather's face was full of wrinkles and resembled a furrowed cornfield about to be planted. His white eyebrows contrasted with his tobacco-colored skin. He also had huge birthmarks, especially on his hands, which resembled the soil. He'd wear a red kerchief on his head and a hat on top. My grandfather was an elegant man. He seemed timeless.

The Story Behind My Name

Now I'm going to tell you a secret. My name isn't really Rigoberta. I know that some of you are going to laugh because I began this story with "my name is Rigoberta." To be honest, my name is and isn't Rigoberta. To clear up the mystery, I'll start at the beginning.

When I was born, my parents gave me my grandmother's name. I was their sixth daughter, and they named me Laj Mi'n. My name changed as I grew up. It was Laj Mi'n when I was little, and Li Mi'n when I wasn't grown up yet and didn't have much understanding about the world. When I am respected and have some knowledge about life, I'll be called Chuch Mi'n. But I am not there yet.

I must admit that Mi'n is a pretty name. Mi'n is one way to say *Domingo* or Sunday in *K'iche'* — a peaceful, relaxed day, the day of the week that is a holiday. That name means having the best in life — the sun, no work, blue sky, games all day, a big lunch in the center of town, no worries at all. Sunday is a sunny, happy and playful day. My true character is like that. I take great pleasure in living. I laugh a lot, tell jokes, kid people.

I'm an optimist who believes that good will triumph over evil. That's why my name is Li Mi'n.

My father registered me late with the mayor's office. When he got there, the clerk asked, "What are you going to call your daughter?"

"Mi'n."

The clerk hadn't heard that name before. He wrinkled his brow, pinched his moustache and adjusted his glasses.

"That name doesn't exist, Don Vicente." (My father's name is Vicente.)

They spent the whole morning arguing.

"It exists," my papá said.

"It doesn't," the clerk countered.

Finally my father gave up, just to comply with the law. "Fine. Mi'n doesn't exist. So what name should I give her?"

The clerk stood up and went over to look at a calendar. It wasn't this year's calendar, but it had pretty pictures. Most important, it had the names of the saints for each day.

"Her name will be Rigoberta, because she was born on St. Rigoberto's Day," the clerk announced. And from that moment on, Rigoberta was my name.

My father came home with the news that my name had changed.

"What's her name now?" they asked him.

"From now on she will be Rigoberta."

Everyone was shocked. They tried to pronounce my new name, which is a bit long. "Ri-go-ber-ta" is as long as the road into town. That's why they started calling me "Beta" here and there. Others called me "Tita." When they got tired of that, they went back to my original name — Laj Mi'n. And at home they all call me Mi'n.

The Story of My Birth

BEFORE BIRTH, we all live in a delicious world. We are in our mother's belly, attached to a little sac called the placenta. We are connected to our mother by an umbilical cord. When we are born, we cry because we are cold. The umbilical cord is cut and we face the world alone.

My mother burned the cord and placenta, so the smoke would be carried up by the winds and form part of Mother Nature's living energy. But she saved part of the cord, which she tied to a string and placed around my neck as if it were a necklace. Two months later it fell off, dried and withered, and was buried in the ground. We do this to give thanks to Mother Earth to whom we belong. It is something sacred. The earth is our mother because she gives us the food that we eat. The earth is our mother because we make our way over her. The earth is our mother because our shadow is always stuck to her. But at the same time, we have our freedom.

We burn the cord and its little companion to be born again. This cord is the only thing that connects me to the life force. We burn the cord to thank nature. Its ashes will form part of

the environment. We also save a piece of the cord to bury in the ground to bind us to it. In this way, Mother Earth will adopt us as her daughter or son. When we must leave the earth, we feel sadness, because part of us stays behind as part of the air, the water, the ground.

When we are born, a little creature is born with us. This creature is just like us. If we sneeze, it sneezes as well, in the forest where it lives. If we sing, it also sings, in its animal language. If we hurt our finger, it will injure a foot, no matter where it is. What happens to us will happen to it. What happens to it happens to us. Sometimes that creature is wiser than we are. It's aware of evil and knows the risks we take, and so it must protect us as it protects itself. That's why we have to respect animals. In Chimel, we call this creature our *nahual*. Each time a child is born, the parents petition their spiritual leaders — *Chuch qajaw*—for the name of the baby's *nahual*. I know mine, but I can't reveal it.

You can have a tiger, a lion, a coyote or a bear as a *nahual*. You can have a puma, a wild boar or a robin redbreast. It can be a swan, a stork or a gazelle. Or it can even be a pig, a mouse or a fox. This doesn't mean that it will be ugly or bad, because there are no ugly or bad animals. All creatures are beautiful. All animals play their role. All animals are good because they help the earth to exist. Without them, we too would cease to exist.

When I Was a Little Girl in Chimel...

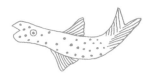

I REMEMBER perfectly our house in Chimel when I was a little girl. It was made out of wood and had a straw roof. I loved to look out between the house slats and see the green fields full of corn, and how the wind stirred them as if they were the long green hair of a woman bathing in the river. I could also see the rabbits in their hutch as they ate their greens — like doctors wearing round glasses and reading a book aloud.

Far in the distance, I could see the river winding through the houses in my village as if it were smoke. On clear days, I could see the high mountains and the sky, the clouds and footpaths — the wide path to Chimel and the narrow path to Laj Chimel.

My brother Patrocinio and I were always together. I must admit that we were a bit naughty.

"Please don't eat the blackberries," our mother would tell us.

And without anyone watching over us, we would go into the fields to pick blackberries. We'd bring with us a chunky, hard brown sugar which we call *panela*.

We'd always eat a few pieces of *panela* with the blackberries.

It was a real feast. We'd go on eating till our bellies hurt. Then we'd return home, with innocent expressions on our faces.

Innocent faces, but our mouths smeared with red. After eating blackberries, our mouths would be red, red, red — like women wearing lipstick.

"You two have been eating blackberries," our mother would scold. And then she'd punish us. What she didn't know was that we had also eaten chunks of brown sugar.

All this happened when I was a little girl in Chimel…

My family cultivated honey. We had six or eight huge honeycombs in the trees, which produced lots and lots of honey. For Holy Week, we would fill up a number of little jars and walk through Chimel giving them away. We'd knock on the doors and say, "Ma'am, we're bringing you a jar of honey."

Our neighbors were very happy, because giving honey away is like giving a bouquet of flowers. It's also like saying something nice or paying someone a compliment or doing a favor. It makes people sweet… It's like giving someone a warm hug.

People want honey. We all want honey.

This happened when I was a little girl in Chimel…

During the rainy season, we would go into the woods to look for mushrooms. Afterward, Mamá would fry them up with garlic, *achiote*, *apazote* or parsley. They were so good you couldn't stop eating them. The only drawback was that picking mushrooms was hard work.

We'd go barefoot with our hair in long braids, like all Maya girls. Since the ground was wet, and there were lots of thorns in the dense mountain forests, any cut on our feet would get infected. As my mother knew herbal secrets, she would wrap our feet in certain leaves so that they'd heal. We'd have to wait for the sun to come out and dry the ground and dry our feet. That's why the other kids would laugh at us and shout,

"Splintered feet, splintered feet, splintered feet!" They would also get "splintered feet" since they too walked about barefoot.

The reward for all this sacrifice was eating those delicious mushrooms. The little mushroom umbrellas would open in the brush, under the trees, damp from so much rain. Some mushrooms were poisonous, while others were sacred. We knew which were sacred, and we wouldn't even touch them. On the other hand, we would pick those that looked like little men walking around with open umbrellas, and eat them with hot tortillas cooked on the griddle above the open fire.

When I was a little girl in Chimel...

Grandfather told us old stories. Mamá would cure our wounds. We'd eat blackberries with brown sugar and give away small jars of honey. Rivers would reflect the sky like a glass snake. The plants were green and abundant and honeycombs were full of bees. The rivers, the swamps, the fields, all of them were full of frogs, toads, crabs and snakes — when I was a little girl in Chimel.

The Curse of the Bees

M Y FAMILY cultivated honey. Honeycombs, brimming with bees, hung from the trees outside, and from them we would get the honey.

At first we had a big tree trunk full of honey. A queen bee in charge of the other bees was in this trunk. When there were too many bees or when there were two queen bees, we would split the swarm and place one of the queen bees and her workers in another honeycomb and hang it from a tree.

Once a queen bee escaped from the honeycomb and got inside our house. We shooed her out and tried to get her to go back to her honeycomb and her hive. But she didn't want to go, and she flew up into the trees. The other bees followed her like a flying black stain, ripping off the leaves with the buzzing of wings.

The next day, the bees from another honeycomb flew off. And then another one. And another one. All the bees were flying off as if they were a squadron of tiny planes. We tried to stop them by making lots of noise with our pickaxes, machetes,

kitchen pots and shovels — anything that could make a racket. That's all we could do to keep them from flying off.

But they paid us no mind. Off they went, drawing an irregular pattern in the sky. Mamá then burned a substance we call *pom,* which we use to ward off evil spirits. Since bees are sacred, their escape could lead to an evil curse. And that's just what happened. But I'm not going to talk about that now. Maybe later.

The Story of the River That Changed Its Course

WHEN I WAS A LITTLE GIRL, a river flowed through Chimel. It wasn't very big, but you could bathe in it, and the women would wash clothes on its large smooth rocks, which resembled giant turtle shells. The women would wash, laugh and talk.

To reach the river, you had to cross a coffee field by going down a narrow little path just wide enough for one person. The coffee field was quite dark because tall trees cast their shadows over it. It was a green darkness full of smells. Sometimes we'd eat the red coffee berries, which had a deliciously sweet taste. Then we'd go down a slope, and the river would appear before our eyes.

The river was crystal clear, like a sheet of cellophane, with the soft gurgle of water. My favorite thing was to jump from stone to stone. The river was miraculous — so much water flowing on and on! It was a gift of nature.

It had lots of little fish, minnows, really. The big fish stayed in deeper water. The river came down from the high mountains, always surrounded by clouds. It ran through the village

and continued till it flowed into the ocean. We never saw the ocean. Papá said that it was huge, as huge as the sky. But I couldn't imagine it.

The little stones in the river were of many colors — orange, green, jet-black, white, amber and yellow. I loved watching them through the lens of the water. I'd put my hand into the water and it would look very big. I would pick up a stone and realize it was tiny. My brothers and I would splash one another until we were completed soaked. Then we'd bathe.

Grandma would say, "You can play in the water as long as you like. But at noon, don't look into the water, especially to the bottom. Your reflection will turn into the shadow of a rooster's face with a greenish blue serpent's tail. And don't stay alone on the river bank because Ajaw, our Maker and Creator, drinks and bathes in the waters of the river."

We learned to swim in the river's coves. Sometimes the current would stop, as if it had gone off on a stroll and was resting near the shore. We would dive off the stones and swim to the river's edge. I remember that we were very happy back then.

The river ran through the village. But when hard times came, when the war began and the villagers had to hide out in the mountains, something magical and unbelievable happened. The river disappeared. It had been so scared by what it had seen in the village during the bad times that it went below the mountain and came out on the other side. And now the river doesn't flow through Chimel.

Together with the villagers, it hid on the other side of the mountain. I would like it to come back. But since a great act of wickedness made it escape, only a great act of kindness can make it come back. Very often I ask myself, what act of kindness could do that? And who would do it?

The Sacred Mountain

CHIMEL is at the foot of a mountain. The village rests against the mountain as if it were a pillow. Whenever I looked up at it, I felt safe. My parents and grandparents told me that it had a soul — a mountain spirit. Since we often climbed it, we'd talk to the spirit before heading out. Nature nourishes us, and for this reason we must respect it.

I loved going up the mountain path, covered with damp leaves. Bit by bit we were in a forest full of very dark green trees and lots of plants and flowers. Fir trees with green needles like Christmas bangles abounded. There were also blackberries, strawberries and raspberries. We'd eat as many as we could and throw the rest into a basket.

I remember all the plum trees. They were very tall. The plum is a delicious oval fruit with a large seed. What most people don't know is that you can eat the leaves of the plum tree. They're not as sweet, but they're very tasty and can make your mouth water.

The birds sang from the trees' tallest branches. The *tukur* or *k'urpup*, the owl, slept up there. It resembled a wise man — the

grandfather of all birds. Sparrows flickered like fleas from branch to branch. Every once in a while a nightingale sang. The swallows would come and go, depending on the season. But there's one bird you saw everywhere — the *sanate,* which imitates the songs of other birds. It's not an evil bird, though it eats the newly planted corn kernels. We consider it a friend, because it's everywhere. Bird song was the music of my childhood.

When we reached the top of the mountain, we'd take out a jug of fresh water and eat tortillas with black beans, guacamole or green peppers. The altitude and fresh air made us very hungry. If there was no fog at the very top, you could see all the valleys and rivers. The plains resembled a yellow, green or red-colored cloth, depending on what had been planted. And off in the distance, like ships sailing between the clouds, you could see the huge Sierra Madre mountain range, with the tips of its volcanoes pointing up to the sky.

When I Was a Girl

Tʜᴀᴛ's ᴡʜᴀᴛ ᴍʏ ʟɪꜰᴇ ᴡᴀꜱ ʟɪᴋᴇ when I was a girl in
Chimel. I remember it was a life of peace and harmony.
We lived in tune with nature. The river bathed and entertained
us. The birds filled our mornings with song. The animals fed us
and gave us company. The mountains protected us, and the
sacred earth gave us the fruits of its womb.

We lived in peace with our village neighbors. The church
was full of worshipers. The women would cover their heads,
and the men would take off their hats. When we had no
priest, my father and other parishioners would read the word
of God.

Our grandparents taught us that the faith and religion
bequeathed to us by our ancestors are not in conflict with any
other faith or religion in the world. Whenever we enter any
temple, we need to respect it with the deepest reverence,
because it is a house of prayer.

Our Maya spiritual guides, the *Chuch qajaw*, conducted our
services with *pom* and ancient village prayers. The men helped
with the chores in the fields. The women gave food and advice

to one another. An elder caressing a head was like a cup of honey in the heart.

Our parents and grandparents showered us with love. This was the most important thing. The love of our relatives and neighbors was given to us and we would return this love. When there were fights, all the villagers participated in determining who was right and who was wrong. And peace was re-established in the village.

My name is Li Mi'n, and I am like a clear and peaceful day — a Sunday — with my heart full of sunlight, happiness in my smile and hope in my head. I long for the days of my childhood — to have a mountain to protect me, a river to refresh me, birds to sing to me.

But I would like everyone, not just me, to have these things. I want the world to be as I remember Chimel.

When I was a girl in Chimel.

GLOSSARY

achiote: red paste derived from the seed of
the bija tree
Ajaw: Maya god
altenxa: herb that cures stomachache
apazote: tropical herb with a strong scent
chilacayote: vegetable that grows on a
climbing vine; its leaves may be used for
healing purposes
chipilín: herb used as a medicine or in
cooking
chiquimula: goldfinch
Chuch qajaw: spiritual leaders or priests
domingo: Sunday
duende: goblin, elf or imp
huipil: woven blouse
k'a q'eyes: cure for viruses such as the com-
mon cold or the flu
K'iche': language spoken by the K'iche'
branch of the Maya in Guatemala

k'urpup: owl
Mi'n: Sunday
nahual: animal spirit, companion
ocote: pitchy wood from the pine tree
panela: pure crystallized sugar from sugar
cane
pom: incense
Popul Vuh: sacred book of the Maya, one
of the oldest books in the Americas
sanate: mockingbird
saq ixog: cure for a range of stomach
ailments
sik'aj: cure for stomach worms
Toj: day when debts are paid in the Maya
calendar
tukur: owl
xew xew: cure for headaches and eye strain
Xib'ab'a: the Maya underworld